A WAY WITH Wild THINGS

Larissa Theule • illustrated by Sara Palacios

BLOOMSBURY
CHILDREN'S BOOKS

NEW YORK LONDON OXFORD NEW DELHI SYDNEY

Poppy Ann Fields liked bugs. They were her friends.

She sat among the wildflowers, listening
patiently to the cicadas' newest symphony.

She coaxed the shy
roly poly out of her shell.

When the ants marched over her,
Poppy let them, even though she was ticklish.

She recognized the spider mama's weaving
for what it was—magnificent art.

And she spent long afternoons talking with the ladybugs about shapes and colors and the heights of flowers.

But when people came around, Poppy preferred to disappear into the background.

At parties she hid in stripes . . .

. . . and in big bright florals.

She became a landscape,

a tree.

She was the pouring rain,

a brocade drape,

a leopard in a menagerie.

When Grandma Phyllis turned 100, Poppy stood watching the party.

Guests milled about, coming together
to hug and shake hands.

Some people danced. Children ran.

They looked like colorful leaves falling
into
each other   then
drifting   apart.

A small wind blew across the garden. On it rode a dragonfly. He landed on the cake. How his wings shimmered in the sun!

Her whole heart glad, Poppy clapped her hands.

Uncle Dan said, **"Poppy Ann Fields, you wallflower, you. So that's where you've been hiding this time."** His voice vibrated louder than a thousand cicadas.

Guests stopped milling about.
Poppy froze.
Every eye fell upon her.
She was scared down to her toes.

The dragonfly flew off the cake . . .

. . . and landed in her hand.

Someone gasped.
"Would you look at that?"
"It flew to her like it knows her."

"Poppy's got a way with wild things,"
said Grandma Phyllis.

Everyone came in for a closer look.

Poppy's feet refused to move. She would have liked to run to the trees beyond the garden. She wished the people would all turn away and leave her alone. She couldn't look at them, so she looked at the dragonfly, soft and fragile in her hands.

She knew the dragonfly had come here for her.
The cicadas' symphony swelled among the trees.
The wind lifted her hair, cooled her face.

She breathed.

"The scientific name is Anisoptera," said Poppy softly, but clearly.

"You wildflower, you," whispered Grandma Phyllis.

The small wind still blew.
Poppy knew she was not a wallflower.
Leaves and wings fluttered to the beat of her heart.
No, not a wallflower . . .

. . . A wildflower.

POPPY'S GLOSSARY OF BUG FRIENDS

 butterfly : friendly; a crooked flier; drinks nectar through a tongue that's like a straw
scientific name: Rhopalocera

 **cicada** : a true bug; makes the loudest music of any insect; vegetarian; after it hatches, it tunnels into the ground to grow
scientific name: Cicadidae

 **dragonfly** : can fly fast, up to thirty miles per hour, and backward; has four delicate, shimmery wings
scientific name: Anisoptera

 ladybug : tiny polka-dot beetle; has hard wings; its bright color and spots scare away predators
scientific name: Coccinellidae

 **praying mantis:** good at camouflage; looks like a stick or a leaf; can be a good pet
scientific name: Manteodea

 **roly poly** : a crustacean, not a bug; shy; lucky to have armor to hide away in if it gets scared
scientific name: Armadillidiidae

 spider : not an insect but an arachnid; eight legs; it weaves webs to catch insects to eat
scientific name: Araneae

For Anya, my wildflower
—L. T.

To my husband, Ed, for not
letting me blend in with the
background anymore
—S. P.

Sara Palacios created the artwork for this book in
layers, with cut paper, acrylic paints, and Photoshop.
Sara loves Poppy because she has always been
shy herself, especially as a little girl, and hopes all
the little wallflowers—*wildflowers!*—out there feel
inspired by this book.

BLOOMSBURY CHILDREN'S BOOKS
Bloomsbury Publishing Inc., part of Bloomsbury Publishing Plc
1385 Broadway, New York, NY 10018

BLOOMSBURY, BLOOMSBURY CHILDREN'S BOOKS, and the Diana logo
are trademarks of Bloomsbury Publishing Plc

First published in the United States of America in March 2020 by Bloomsbury Children's Books

Text copyright © 2020 by Larissa Theule · Illustrations copyright © 2020 by Sara Palacios

Bloomsbury books may be purchased for business or promotional use. For information on bulk purchases
please contact Macmillan Corporate and Premium Sales Department at specialmarkets@macmillan.com

Library of Congress Cataloging-in-Publication Data
Names: Theule, Larissa, author. | Palacios, Sara, illustrator.
Title: A way with wild things / by Larissa Theule ; illustrated by Sara Palacios.
Description: New York : Bloomsbury, 2020.
Summary: Poppy Ann Fields loves bugs and feels more comfortable outdoors than with other
people until a special bug lands on Grandma Phyllis's birthday cake. Includes a glossary of insects.
Identifiers: LCCN 2019019153 (print) | LCCN 2019021852 (e-book)
ISBN 978-1-68119-039-6 (hardcover)
ISBN 978-1-68119-040-2 (e-book) · ISBN 978-1-68119-041-9 (e-PDF)
Subjects: | CYAC: Insects—Fiction. | Bashfulness—Fiction.
Classification: LCC PZ7.T3526 Wi 2020 (print) | LCC PZ7.T3526 (e-book) | DDC [E]—dc23
LC record available at https://lccn.loc.gov/2019019153

Typeset in Sassoon Sans Std
Book design by Jeanette Levy
Printed and bound in China by Leo Paper Products, Heshan, Guangdong
2 4 6 8 10 9 7 5 3 1

All papers used by Bloomsbury Publishing Plc are natural, recyclable products
made from wood grown in well-managed forests. The manufacturing
processes conform to the environmental regulations of the country of origin.

To find out more about our authors and books
visit www.bloomsbury.com and sign up for our newsletters.